I0552694

Gnarly Roots

Jack Kolkmeyer

Delray Beach, Florida
2018

Forte Publishing

First Published in 2018
Published by:

FORTE Publications
#12 Ashmun Street
Snapper Hill
Monrovia, Liberia
[+231] 777155-923
[+231] 881-106-177

FORTE Publishing
7202 Tavenner Lane
208 Alexandria
VA, 22306

FORTE Press
76 Sarasit Road
Ban Pong, 70110
Ratchaburi, Thailand
[+66] 85-824-4382

http://fortepublishing.wix.com/fppp
fortepublishing@gmaill.com

Printed in the United States of America

ISBN-13: 978-0-6481823-5-1

Dedication

To all who dig deeply

Introduction

Gnarly Roots is the third book in a series that explores the challenges of being aware on our planet and in the cultural realms in which we live our lives.

Higher Glyphics examined the **mysteries** around us and our searching for their meanings and their relationships to our personal lives. What are the pyramids, henges, hieroglyphics, petroglyphs? What are their messages to us in these times?

A Philosophy of Yard focused on **understanding** how we grasp the world around us, its mysteries and magic, and how we view ourselves, where we come from in our thinking, and how we are grounded.

Gnarly Roots is about our **entanglements**. Our lives are full of complications, knots and swirling issues. Untangling the knots and resolving the complications can be Gordian, for sure. These entanglements can be social, spiritual, financial, political, personal... doesn't matter.

We all strive, in some regard, to untangle.

Contents

the first knowings
      are often just diminutive notions
a flurry of pass
perhaps owing to a loftier moment
      of integration
      of several points of view
that you may not have expected
      and therefore
       ever considered

but now
in the dealings of this current specter
      you become aware
      of the larger proportions
      of potential conflict
of segregation
of the soul and the spirit
      from the importance
      of the little motions

that constantly grow around you
and therefore

always need to be considered

gnarly roots

the gnarly roots of the old
banyan tree
desperately scratch
        at the ground
        in an age old attempt

to claw their way
    to the heavens

while branching out
        shades the anxiety of the search
        and provides shelter
        from the storms and respite
        to the gamely fights and scars
        that always transpire underneath

the real arboreal aspiration
is manifest in the elder entanglements of girth
and the trunk full of treasures
buried in the earth

as the roots stay firmly grounded
      to support the timeless expansion
      of the natural urge to spread higher

and of our constant wondering

just when will we find
      the ancient star seeds
      that planted us here

in the first place

from the ground up

from down looking up
you get to see all of the roots
and foundations
        of so many splendid structures
        and undertakings
so many footsteps in the ochre dust
        blown into reclusiveness
        by winds of changes in the
climate
        of all that surrounds us

sitting on the cooling grass
in the appreciated moisture
        of early Spring
you see intensity and aspiration
        in all aspects of the much
layered terrain
setting forth abundance
and ingenuity
        and of course
there are many hustlings that don't
make sense on the ground
        but have a very balanced notion
when seen from above at a wider angle

how tributaries work
and just how far away volcanic spew
    can slap its molten handprint
    on many of these hillsides
facing us

but from where we stand
the vision is mutely etched into the cliff
side
    with a panoramic sweep of land
so full of life
    and death
and sweeping opportunity
one of personal expanse
    and hopeful anticipation in concert
with
    the inspiration and wisdom of the
seasons
and understanding the reason why
withering away
    is just a part of being ground up

and as always
knowing when to hide

a bee convention

there's a bee convention
    down at the first orange blossom
    of the season
a gathering of early morning honey
dews
    abuzz with the news of a sweet
reason
to hang out and suck on the beauty of
life

the mixing of exaltation with intention
    has a way of twisting reality and
illusion
    to spring forth a different nectar
that appears to thrive on hints
of coming changes

so they hum along from bloom to
bloom
    spreading rumors among their pollen
friends
    until they have visited the entire yard
    and every flower
    even sharing secrets with the
hummingbirds

    all of them working so hard
    jestering in the wind
    until it ends
    as it always does
    with a shower of abject sweetness

a choice in the wilderness

if you put your ear to the ground
  you can hear it
  when you put your finger to the wind
  you can feel it
  just set your eyes to the sky
  and you can see it

  it might sound like a voice
  or a rustle in the restless breeze
  like a battered flag of allegiance
  or appear as a dancing spectral illusion
of trickery

  but in reality

  if you just stand still and wait
  for just less than a bristling moment
  until the illusive penumbra of doubt
  has shredded itself into the
disconnected shards
  of forgotten dreams

scattering into the forlorn stretches
    of old desiccated desires and dog-eared wants

it settles on you like the dawn
    skidding into dusky exasperation
    through the hole in a gorget around
antiquity

that it is cause for rejoice

it is not a mirage of some forgotten time
    chanting highly charged ohms to the
sublime
    in subtle tones of longing

it is the precise acknowledgement
you have been waiting for
it is a choice in the wilderness

crying out to be chosen

the nesting place

waking up in this nest we call home
    the first attention is to the protection
    of this humble little place
    nestled in the strong arms
    of our familiar neighborhood
    that branches out from here to there
the boundaries that we all respect
and care for

we know there are fly by nights
who would steal from us

    snatching a meal from the very mouths
    of our offspring
    we can sense invaders and know well
    those who are not from here
    or who at least share a kindred spirit
    with our kind
keeping an eye on them is of concern to all
and to some we assign the duty to be on
the look out
      in all directions
just in case

then we turn to food
    at times an easy snatch from scattered seeds
other times
a chase among the obstacles and weeds
    for that elusive but tasty morsel

then our fancy turns to frolic and fun
    chasing each other and nipping at the
feathers
    or the fuzz of our family and friends

    and finally to the freedom to soar
    winging way above the confines of our
place
    to find a new face to float with and
    to find new realms and hear new songs
    beyond the tones of ours

    but
    someone from the place up the road
    from that strange roost perching on the
ground
    just put up a barrier that winds its way
    all around

a rake's head

the width of your garden path
    should be enough for the head of a
rake to swipe through
    so that you can sweep your way clear
of detritus
    and fallen leaves
    left by the winds of change
    and made moist by the rains of
torment
and need

when your garden path becomes cluttered
    and impassable
    it might become impossible to tend
    the fruits of your labor
    and the nourishment of your soul
    that you planted in the hope
of harvesting some juicy moments

if you can see your way clearly
into your carefully cultivated garden of
    earthly delights

you will enjoy the strawberry smiles
and broadly shouldered might of the
    collards
and smell the aromatic allure of thyme
well spent

you can pause amidst the flowering sage
and hear the rabbit heartbeats
left behind
just for you

because you etched your garden path
enough for the head of a rake
to pass through

birds of a nether

birds of a nether
    stalk the nesting of innocent watchers
    together
to stuff their mouths
    with phony words
and empty paraphrasing

they fly around
in blazing frocks of darkness
    together
flashing their downward lilt
    and pompous vigor
    always to insinuate

pecking is the order of their day
    as there is no other way
    to determine the elders from the youth
    together
as they squawk and ruffle feathers
    among themselves

but they capitulate

waiting on the wires
    for another moment
    together

to strike back at the starkness
    of guilt and feathered illusion

    and flights of fancy

    together
    the birds of the nether

droplet

a small pool of water
    is an ocean
    to the less than gargantuan

a puddle perhaps
    but a submersive point of view
    for those who choose to jump
    into this reflective place

or a torrential storm
    when the droplets turn
    their temperament to a more
    destructive intent

    ballistic in its change of function

and naturally there are the springs
    and the waterfalls
    where tranquility is a rainbow
    in the mist
    of so much falling water

and so the rivers flow
    with the strength and fortitude
    of commonality and confluence
    drop by drop
    into the valleys
    that funnel them
in to our needs

but then there is that singular drip
    seemingly from nowhere
    that splats on your nose
and drops down to somewhere
    beneath you
    for

even a droplet
    can turn the tide
    of the tiny

frozen in time

the cold from down there
always brought up stories from another
time

    images that conjured warmer moments
    and shifting colors that vibrated
    with sound so different from footprints

    in an oddly present way
    curving the visions of sky watching
    to understand the grounding of the
cold

    the big shift came as no surprise
    with its arcing tail of flame
    scouring our pathways of coexistence
and creating the current state
of collective mental drift

that's what happens when
fire and ice collide

a great rift rends the crust of civilization
into shards of escape and torment
into stone fractures and forgotten speak

from cold
to hot
to warm
the cycles turn in timely
precession glides

and so we come and go
magnificence to ice
in slides of dust and ash
the credence and intelligence burned
into mythic embers of illusion
that glow and flicker
as they always fall once again
into the finely blended mix
of cultural amnesia and ground up spirits
such is the story of falling fire
and how ice ages

frozen in time warps
as time goes by

Eclipse My Soul

The Solar Eclipse
August 21, 2017
Buena Vista, Colorado

crossing the lines
and blurring the visions
as the circles recycle
    from the light to the dark
    and back again
    ebullient to stark

an eclipse is a lunar journey
to another side
of the welling up of emotions
    entangling star studded mysteries
    with mythic understandings
    here, there and all around

dropping by momentarily
  to deliver the word
        and the messages
        from outer realms
        in a different shine

  we forever mark these movements
  in the circles of our minds

  and the stones that we plant
  all around and
        in mounds
        as memories
        on the ground

heal thyself

to heal yourself
   of whatever ails you
delve deep inside your body realms
   into the patch of inner garden
that requires tending

there
turn the soil of your soul
   with the prodding fingers of your mind
asking for providence and guidance
   from those who thrive there with you
   and who understand how to dig
deeper into
the hidden layers and underworlds
of this subcutaneous land

for they can lend their knowledge
   and many hands
   to restructuring the potential bounty
of your body harvest
and cure those momentary maladies

from the inside out

horizontal

the horizon
is a majestic plain ride

a peacock's tale spun above the terrain
of our daily discourse
beginning stories of deep aspiration
and common cause

unfolding

an odyssey of timeless adventure
and thrilling escape

speeding across the escarpment of hope

a shifting float of colored swipes
and momentary bluster

that never ends

every day

the little nun

she walks by each morning

the little nun
    from the cloister down the road
held up in her lofty aspirations by all of
the mysteries
    entangled beneath her

Sculpture: Les Météores. By Nadine Fourré

la petite nonne

elle se promène chaque matin

la petite nonne
    depuis le cloître en bas de la route
tenue dans ses nobles aspirations de tous
les mystères
    enchevêtrés sous elle

la pequeña monja

ella camina por las mañanas

la pequeña monja
    desde el claustro por el camino
sostenido en sus nobles aspiraciones de
todos los misterios
    enredado debajo de ella

The Faces of Elder Wisdom

the faces of elder wisdom
bear a visage of know and how
    and see with eyes of then and now
they hear with whispers of the wind
    and the delight of bird song

the faces of elder wisdom
bare no grudges
    their wrinkles are but chasms of time
facial landscapes of earth melody
and people rhyme

the faces of elder wisdom
reach out their arms
    beyond the confines of them
into moments of teach
and respectful reach

the faces of elder wisdom
walk into the face of adversity
    and sit among the aches of diversity
to speak with words
    that charm and inspire

the faces of elder wisdom
are mirrors of you and me
    as we walk the same pathways
and sit around the same shared fires
    that send our thoughts and
aspirations
to lofty places
so much calmer

the faces of elder wisdom
teach us that

Pining Away

morning sweat still nestles
on the pine needle clusters
   of kindred green

as the blue birds squawk
   their early territory squabbles
   about a small shift in the winds
   or their equally hungry aviatic friends
   or
   just some other unknown wings
   always seemingly on their bird brains

the small needled ones
gather round their long cone keepers
   whispering to each other
and singing their resin toned praises

to the rising sun

but it is the long needled royalty
that stick their poses

into the morning light
and reign adorningly
over all the others
for even the elders know
the rule of the pines

flowers glow in their direction
and a sweet little rush of thrushes
    thrives inside a clutch of branches

while a stand of nearby aspens whisper
    softly intoned melodies
    in slipping harmonies
    with the river flow

and all is always ever green
in the midst of the morning reflections
    of blue on blue

here pining away
in the natural realm of resins

on the other hand

on the one hand
it's very simple

on the other
it's even beyond astrology
    into the nethers
    of spirit searching
and soul destiny

still

on another hand
it's right here
    staring you in the face

it becomes a matter of

seeing
    and believing
tracing
    an understanding
hearing
    a knowing

and
    of course, feeling

and having the courage
to shake hands and grow up

footnotes

you can take a chance

realizing that after the first step
   into another realm

there are infinite combinations
for you to follow

so you can step lightly
   or dance with abandon

   that decision is inherent

in the rhythms you choose

fire
the original tool of willful people

    the light of light
    the light of love

Prometheus found it
Vulcan pounds it

your love expounds it
your death grounds it

build a fire

higher
    and higher
    and higher

embraceable you

come
put your harms around me
so we can delve into them
    one by one
looking for clues to unlock the gates
    of repressed passageways
leading into the inner realms
    of our anxieties and misgivings

then
we can throw down our amulets
and charms
and once and for all
dispel any notions of misinterpretation
    of the signs we have followed
    or the messages
we firmly believe were given to us
    incorrectly
    or unknowingly

so come embrace me
    and these moments of change
    and these times of fearfulness

hold tightly
   on to the truths that have guided you
   to this point

hold them close to your heart
   until your blood runs warm
with their deep meaning
   and intimate fervor

and then
unclasp them and watch them fly
   into the face of delusion
soaring beyond the culturally crafted
   webs of illusion

into the grasp of nothingness

into the arms of the true embrace

that only knows

freedom

ankh you

it is always beneficial to carry
an amulet with you
    when traveling the spaceways
    or the highways and byways
    for that matter

it's why St. Christopher dangles
from so many mirrors
    looking forward and backward
    for your well being

the same reason applies to why
    there are so many biblical crossings
    davidic or charismatic
and why

scapulars and passport masks
    accompany the saints
    and the sojourners

that lucky penny in your pocket
    flattened on the train tracks
    behind the house
    reminds you of the good
    that is yet to come

on all the walks of life
helping to protect and aid
in the battles and strife we encounter
    along the way

the rabbit's foot
    that always seems to walk away
    when you need it most

    but of all the charms that come your way
    it's the ankh on the wall

that shimmers most mysteriously
    when the sun comes up
    and then again when it sets
    and emits that ancient ray

that hits you in the eye
and sets your soul on fire

doin' it

at some point that turns in life
that your life turns on
you come to realize
that you just have to do it

you simply have to jump for joy
    and to conclusions that were
sometimes a barrier
to the path that you desired
in the first place anyway

but you had to shift for a moment or two
into the realms of learning and
responsibility
    and parenthood and desperate
obligation
in order to work your way through
a schedule of some sort
that you or someone
    thought was important to follow

and so you did

with satisfaction to a remote corner
of your soul
    and to innate heart beats that guided
    or misguided the intentions
that you perceived were intended for you

now

as you look into the mirrored
remembrances of your past
into the softly focused aspirations
of your future

you realize that it is time

to just go do it

sun flowers

a small village of sunflowers
resides
in the south corner of the garden

the doves drove them there
on their wings of dawn
    a direct flight from the green feeder
    hanging temptingly
    on a mango tree branch

to a newly turned
    ground unit
    with a view

they have added another distinct
voice to the choral arrangements
already well-practiced in their lofty soil
choirs

and so they blend their floral tones
rooted in their dirt bones

and sing along

beaming

studying
a sly smile of moon
settle into the sultry embrace
     of early morning light pulses
          peeking over the furtive glimpses
of the phantom mountains in the mist

watchfully overlooking
this ancient spirit home

wondering
just how soon
the dawn fingers
     will scratch a new unknown image
     into the raw tonal skin
     of change

on another daily face

blamin' the shaman

they can't be real and tangible
the dreams of shamans
    because they do not fit squarely
    into the geometric notions
    of rightfulness

they must be phantasms of hatred and
resentment
    for why else would they want to be a
jaguar
    lurking in the jungles of night pulse
    and wanting to rip to shreds the
gnawing
    clutches of impending cultural
intrusions

just why would they snort those mud
induced elixirs
    to venture so far off the path of
accepted ways
and talk in garbled voices that only seem
to have meaning
    in the realms of nothingness
and dance to tunes so distorted that the
melodies

are only sung by bugs and beetle
groups

try explaining to me in common phrases then
    how the lesions of regret and despair
    heal so easily with their balms of leaf
knowledge
and how they can extend themselves so
deeply into the hallucinogenic
    worlds of eerie voices and shifting shapes
    that help them understand the
misunderstandings
    of currently alternating points of view
 and still come back to smile at us
in disbelief

don't spite the herb that needs you
don't blame the shaman
for being the messenger

just follow the hart
    into the deep
    of the forest ways
    in plain sight

corner stones

comprehending the magnitude of
megalithic structures
and the depth of piling cultures one upon
another
for the embrace of the gods and goddesses
of lost eras
shrouded in hidden hopes and dreams
remains an unlodged mystery of geometric
entanglements

still the answer is the same
as one culture builds upon the ashlars of
another
and an old deity bends into a new faith
rising from the fire and ashes
of ancient internments sparking embers
    of twisted tongues
for which the meaning is obscured
or now simply made up
to fit the new hopes of present punctures
into the vellum of then

so in reality

what we adore in the simple celebration of time

torqueing tortuously from one permutation
to the next
are more than just primeval mounds of passing
but are culturally significant circular chapters
    in the many layered stories of our fore
bearings

it makes sense to assume that somewhere
resting maternally covered in reverence
is the mother lode of all
waiting patiently to bear the womb mates
to help us raise anew another lithic hope

as watchers and architects of understanding
the blurred visions
etched into the corner stones of time
we appear to go back and then forward
as the winds of change divert us
from place to place
until we rest again in the cradle of antiquity
under the symbols rising from the rubble
of the foundations of ruin
that once themselves were sprinkled with
the stones that fell
from heaven

axis

the wizened old banyan
    embedded in our front yard
is more than just an arching entryway
    into our home

she is
as some of our more established denizens
    have acknowledged
the axis of our neighborhood universe

as she shoots her offspring
    into the ground
and spreads her gracefully gnarled arms
    under the sheltering canopy
that is the nesting and resting place
    of numerous animal people
    and surreal creatures of the fired
imagination
always relishing
in the peeking sun, the moon glazing and
the star spokes

that spirit the beliefs
    of all of us
who encounter her or live within her
penumbra

we spin around her daily
with the wind and rain
    and the passing of days
    and the whisper of falling leaves
riding in and out of her seasonal embraces

lightning shies away
    in deference to a telephone pole
even the bellicose fury of hurricanes
    sifts through her maze of branches
    with a humbling regard

and so she holds her ground
establishing her positon as both
    royalty
    and
the axis of our very existence

Ages of Rocks

long ago
they were cast into these streams
as molten geologic memory stones
rippling spells of our physical
consciousness

falling downward from the uplifts of time
and the volcanic emotions of long ago
dropping piece by piece
fragment by filament
floating lithic parchments
becoming alluvial shards
in a watery embrace of glacial melt
seeking their own unique course

so here
they now rest
sit for a moment
perhaps an eon
some as stoic as the day they emerged
others
    newly sculpted

by the rays of generations
or the winds of constant shift

whatever their birthright
or sudden flight
their presence
is now artistically augmented
by the sheen
of their crystalline faces
the glint of sun times and moon glare
the constant massage of liquid fingers
the shatter of lightning impulses
or the slide of unwelcome mountain
visitors

there are those who shatter
with passing surges
to disperse their angular glisten
along their shoulders
and so we uncover them and solemnly
place them in smaller cairns

along the shores
    to remind them just how far
    they have flung their flowing
knowledge

but still
    they sit
the rocks of ages
bathing in their eddies of fish delight
steadfast
    in their roll of surge
as reminders of days gone by
into the entrapment of a present tense

waiting
for the future urge
    of new earthly changes
    and evolutionary rhymes in lime tones
    and schistic vibrations

to roll on

plant speak

yes
it's true
plants do speak

it takes some time to learn
their windborne pollen tongue
and grasp how they petal along the syntax
of their nature ways
and to grasp the images that they use
and the allusions they make
but if you listen
you can hear

for just like us
they bear the stigma of their creation
that they pass along in bee lines
from one filament of their growth
to another
until their story blooms
in radiant manifest
resting on the pedestal of their roots
they grow, mature and retire
happily chatting among their compatriots
on the plantations
of evolution
August Eclipse 2017, Buena Vista, CO

black tree

the steadfast obsidian tree

stood with folded arms

a eunuch in the weeds

suddenly

bull dozed

Athens, Ohio

leaves

a magenta leaf
from a flowering bougainvillea

    sees an opening among
the reddish marigolds

and carefully pedals
its way
into the floral pastiche

Delray Beach

The Palm Wine Drinkard
Uh Wunjuka Tunungee*
For Amos Tutuola
*(Kpelle of Liberia : my head is turning)

like beer
palm wine is an acquired taste
some like it, some don't

it's a native thing too
because not everyone has piassava trees
    growing in their back yards
it's not like running to the super market
for a cold six pack

if you want to do it the local way though
it's a musky morning meeting
    an adventure in the dawn light
climbing the tree
tapping the serious vein
getting the gourd just right

so they asked me along
to tap the tree
work on the farm for a bit

and then seal the deal
with a calabash full
of rainforest honey dew
on our way back into the village

climbing the tree was easy
the pot was full of briny palm wine
    with a smattering or two of flies
    easily shooed away

we imbibed the milky drink
    strong and earthy thick
but before long
my head was spinning
    the ground disappeared from sight
they laughed

not sure exactly how we got back home
they said my legs were long
    and my head had turned
into another deep forest world

several sages

there are several sages rooted in the
garden

they may not appear to be who you
might think they should be
      draped in their coats of many colors
      perfumed with the essence of thyme
and coiffed in hand wrung curly parsley braids

oh no
underneath it all
they are slender stalks of amaizement
      the luxurious aloe vera healing hands
      embracing the wise fingers of
rosemary
and always the prescient comings and
goings of sage

to nurture and prolong them
you just add buckets of holy water
      and sufficient moments of adoration
and attention
      to the gentle soil in which they plant
themselves
and find their footing

but beware the basilisk
    who glides among the lower depths
    in stealthy maneuvers
to gain respect for ways not readily accepted

the quest is up to them
    to guide you and attract more acolytes
to serve the ways and means
of wisdom seekers

think of them perhaps as asterisms
    sparkling among the splendors of the
trees of life
preserving our movements forward
    to a more comprehensive
understanding
of it all

sitting in our garden of thought
    among the sages on the edge
conjuring the flora sprites to come and chat
    about how to make new places
where the heavens meet the earth

as it is written on the garden stones

staying on the path

we often share a notion
that staying on the path
    takes us safely to our destinations

but sometimes

we also share the wrath
of unexpected motions
    that quickly swerve us
    into new exotic realms
outside the confines of our imaginations

there are so many comforting knowns
along the way
    that build the edifice complex
    that guides our journey along
familiar country roads and along the
elegant boulevards of experience

but then
there are the unknowns
the back alleys and side streets
    and perceived short cuts
    that always appear to parallel
our urge to be different

and so

the problem with the pathways
is significant
    then and now
whether to stay
    or whether to stray
either by choice or by force of nature
from those disruptive times and events
    that veer us off and change the
course of us
    without consent and absolutely no remorse

and we are faced with the decision
    to revision a new connection
through unfamiliar terrain
where we now wander and search
    for new uncertain locations
    where we are obliged
to rebuild our sacred tombs and holy domes
    and relocate the old domains
    that people our lives

for that is the way the path now points
    the only way that remains

coming or going

some dream of flights of fancy
    into ethereal spirit realms
    or off into far off
fanciful worlds

others of us
want to stay put

cruising at the helm
    of a voyage that unfurls
    before us
and following a course
    of action
that we inherited
here
    and are just simply
taking it all
for granite

systemic wandering

looking out the window of opportunity

you see past adventures that you undertook
because you thought about them for an eternity
    and knew the chance would come your way
    with a bit of certainty and repetition of
intention
if not in fact just eons of patience

other dreams
took an impetus of very dry kindling
    and years of fire in the belly
    of the wailing desires
    deep into long and restless night flights
    of rumination and constant rearranging
    of the order of the steps that you were sure
had footing in apparent opportunity
    to bring them into the light
    of convinced reality
    but
other journeys you just never take

or
have the time to get to

The Drum is the Voice of the Trees

the drum
    is the voice of the trees
you taste its lilt on your hips
and hear its heartbeat
    in the breeze

the drum
    gives us roots music
    and trunk space
    and leaf scatter
    and branch breaking
as a symbol
of love and a constant steady rainfall

the drum
    is the choice of the trees
    with all due respect to fiddling around
    and basic intentions

for the drum
    keeps us up late
    watching stars and flying embers

it makes us other worldly specters
half-baked with an urge
from the heat of dancing
and then
the drum walks us home
with a surety and sprightliness of step
and not ironically
well, perhaps iconically
right on time
to watch the moonglow
melt into the morning notes
coming from the birds and the
churches

yes, you see

the drum
is the voice of the trees
because

the drum
is the choice of the trees

In the Garden of Earthly Delights

a flurry of pollen words
buzz around the glistening ears of corn

listening

for directives from the more seasoned
ones

the potato eyes the subterranean
    lurkings of an underground harshness

onions set the tone for the course
    of the conversation that grows here
as a pungency of pepper
    adds a spice to the mix of daily finds

the carrot tops enjoy
the gleeful surprise of bunching
    up against certain beans
    that can string together all of

the ingrained
        understandings of the soil
        and its soul mates
without hesitation

as the garlic bulbs light the way
and a gentle rain washes away any
harshness
that lingers over the garden of earthly
delights

to remind us
        of the beauty
        and the bounty
all around us

today

        and, hopefully,
        tomorrow as well

the heard mentality

if you choose to be sucked into the
maelstrom of sameness
be of mind that it is not a current to
freedom
    but a plunge into the finality of falsely
spoken words
    of ideologies gone astray

words have a way of morphing over time
    and meanings can become smirched
    with the slang and barbs of erratic wisdom
and the diversions of truncated belief systems
    designed to herd you aboard ismatic ships
    that sail far beyond their ports of origin
    especially when written in a language
    long lost among the towers of babble
that align themselves along the twisted ways
    but still mark the settlements that housed
the true meanings of our beginnings

as the watchers over words gone awry
we must look beyond the syntax of this
unjust sentence
    to the confines of the moment's mediocrity
    into the realms of gnostic expansion
    and stellar teachings that only require
us to look up

and down more deeply into the soul of
ossified lost times

compare that to the stagnant phrases of now
     and reparse your hearing to the
revisions of the wind
     and once again to the constellations
that align the night skies

so if you come as a messenger to bring
enlightenment
     to the darkest fractals of times
     be prepared to accept that your
message may rile the sentiments of
power and greed controlling our strained ideals
and limit the knowing of these times
because if the message is pure
in its tone and intention
     it will rise above the sediments of
hate and destruction
and allow for the prosper of reconstruction
     of the temple of understanding
     of who we are
where we come from and where we must go
     in our quest to fit into the foundation
of layered antiquity
and into the nature of it all

entanglements

there are always
    a couple of ways
    to deal with and untangle
even the most formidable
    and gnarly of knots

with one fierce downward slash
    of a desperately acerbic tongue
the ball of nots
    can quickly be cut into perfect halves
reflecting on what they used to entwine

or

a set of sharply honed fingers
    with the patience of an era

can slowly but efficiently
    undo what also took a long time to
do
long ago and far away

knots are akin to roots
not unlike a saxophone is to flutes

as the notes and knots of entanglement
    are a constant ritualistic weave of
innate patterns
    and desires

meant to always be a mystery
to be resolved by someone
    who deeply wants

to know

the great primordial mound

the depth of the arrangement of the
earthen mounds
and pyramid structures
    that have piled one culture upon
another
        embracing the gods and goddesses
        of civilizations blinked away

remain an unresolved mystery
of both geometric and philosophical
distortions
    fragmented by the broken mirrors of
hope
        and awkwardly imaged dreams

still

the answer to the question of deepness
is the same

one culture generates another
    building on the detritus of forgotten
deities
one god leads to another
    one goddess rises from the wings of
one before

so in the reality of now
what we adore is the simple celebration of
time
    slipping from one realm into another
    rising out of the ashes of lost
remembrances
leaving behind mounds of buried
truthfulness

it makes sense though
to assume that somewhere along the line
    is the mother of all mounds
    resting under the winds of change
    that divert us from place to place
until we lose sight of the nest
    cradled in the breast of antiquity

over time
the symbols sprout up again
    from beneath the rubble
into the glorious steadfast foundations
that are the mighty stones
    of majesty
along the unending shores
    of creation

time is running out

at times

it feels like time is running out
dripping like a surreal clock
    around the edges of reality
    on to the pathways of familiarity
one drop at a time

other times of course

as you work through hourly endeavors
    and day turnings of free will
    you can only implore
that time stand still

and then

there are the time capsules and the corner
stones
    intended to capture storied moments
    for posterity of some future relevance
only to be entombed themselves

but

as time would have it
time never runs out

time

is the minute internal clock
of infinity

second to none

the vernal equinox

on the first day of Spring
we burn the branches of the Yule fir
        the steadfast pine that brought us
winter
        and becomes the daring harbinger
of shift
a practice that our grandmother taught us
        long ago and far away in the garden
we grew together in
        a remembrance from old Teutonic
times
that somehow still resides in our star
crossed genes
and infinite bloodline gifts

lighting the aromatic sprigs
with a spark of new intention
        ignites a spiraling wisp of
smoldering greens
        that meanders its way up to the
morning lunar melt
        and glaring solar gleams
that stare upon this morning
        of yet another change in the daily
chapters
still yearning to be read

the insect eyes and birding dreams
alight along the flames
    as the little beasts of night and day
    assemble to watch the animistic rituals
    and listen to the timely chants
    and monotheistic prayer calls
as they know what's up and still ahead
    and what goes down on days like this
    for they've been abuzz and singing all along
as the daffodils nod their heads
and bud into the surging song

so once again as if it were a deified plan
we shift the planet gears
    from winter's bare necessities
to the warming of the embers
    now hissing their siren songs that
swirl above

melding as if it were an ancient rhyme
        into the morning church bell chimes
        that call the angelic spirits to us
to come gather round
the soaring fire
that greets the vernal equinox
now springing from the ground

75

Threesome

three deep roots
merge
into this corporeal arrangement
    that we call
our home life

the terrestrial implant
about keeping your feet on the ground
    and always trying to
move along

there's the middle road
and the ever groaning of the groin
    in its constant lament
for more pleasure and nourishment

and then there's the head liner
    with its beaming pineal eye
    forever searching the heavens for
mystery

and more answers

to timeless
questions

About The Author

Jack Kolkmeyer studied English Literature/ Creative Writing at Ohio University in the 1960's where he developed a special interest in the Romantic, Imagist and Beat poets. He was the Editor of *Sphere*, the Ohio University literary magazine, from 1967-68. His writings have appeared in numerous publications including *The Writers Place* and *The Liberian Literary Magazine* and have been broadcast on his popular Santa Fe radio programs, *The International House of Wax* and *Brave New World*, and presented with his performance group, The Word Quartet. Jack currently reads his works on Brave New World and The Tone Age, two programs on his internet radio station, Fifthwall Radio.

He was a Peace Corps Volunteer in Liberia, West Africa from 1969-72 and was greatly influenced then by the emerging African writers of that time, especially Leopold Senghor, Chinua Achebe and Amos Tutuola. Jack received an MPA in Public Policy/Urban and Regional Planning from Indiana University in 1974.

Jack moved to Santa Fe, New Mexico in 1975 to study filmmaking at The Anthropology Film Center and worked there professionally in city planning, education, broadcasting and the performing arts, and journalism. Jack currently resides and writes in Delray Beach, Florida where his current writing projects include poetry, music and city planning topics, and screenplays.

www.ingramcontent.com/pod-product-compliance
Lightning Source LLC
Chambersburg PA
CBHW072019170626
46813CB00005B/2185